Cloud Capers

SUE BENTLEY

Illustrated by Angela Swan

GROSSET & DUNLAP
Published by the Penguin Group
Penguin Group (USA) Inc., 375 Hudson Street, New York, New York 10014, USA
Penguin Group (Canada), 90 Eglinton Avenue East, Suite 700,
Toronto, Ontario M4P 2Y3, Canada
(a division of Pearson Penguin Canada Inc.)
Penguin Books Ltd., 80 Strand, London WC2R 0RL, England
Penguin Group Ireland, 25 St. Stephen's Green, Dublin 2, Ireland
(a division of Penguin Books Ltd.)
Penguin Group (Australia), 250 Camberwell Road, Camberwell,
Victoria 3124, Australia
(a division of Pearson Australia Group Pty. Ltd.)
Penguin Books India Pvt. Ltd., 11 Community Centre, Panchsheel Park,
New Delhi—110 017, India
Penguin Group (NZ), 67 Apollo Drive, Rosedale, North Shore 0632, New Zealand
(a division of Pearson New Zealand Ltd.)
Penguin Books (South Africa) (Pty.) Ltd., 24 Sturdee Avenue,
Rosebank, Johannesburg 2196, South Africa

Penguin Books Ltd., Registered Offices:
80 Strand, London WC2R 0RL, England

Text copyright © 2008 Sue Bentley. Illustrations copyright © 2008 Angela Swan. Cover
illustration copyright © 2008 Andrew Farley. First printed in Great Britain in 2008 by Penguin
Books Ltd. First published in the United States in 2009 by Grosset & Dunlap, a division of
Penguin Young Readers Group, 345 Hudson Street, New York, New York 10014. GROSSET &
DUNLAP is a trademark of Penguin Group (USA) Inc. Printed in the U.S.A.

Library of Congress Cataloging-in-Publication Data is available.

ISBN 978-0-448-45046-9   10 9 8 7 6 5 4

To Ziggy—four-squat and ugly-cute,
but full of character.

Prologue

Storm, the young silver-gray wolf, barked with fear as a terrifying howl rose on the icy air and echoed over the dark mountain.

"Shadow!" Storm gasped.

The fierce lone wolf, who had killed Storm's father and three litter brothers and wounded his mother, was very close.

There was a dazzling bright flash and a shower of gold sparks. Where Storm had been standing there now crouched a tiny Jack Russell puppy with soft brown-and-white fur, a white tail, and midnight-blue eyes.

Storm hoped this disguise would protect him. He leaped toward a clump of snow-covered rocks, his tiny puppy heart beating fast. He needed to find somewhere to hide—and quickly.

"In here, my son," growled a soft velvety voice.

Storm plunged deeper into the shadows and ran toward the she-wolf who was slumped beneath a rocky shelf. He recognized his mother immediately and he licked his mother's muzzle.

Canista reached out a large silver paw and drew the small puppy against her thick warm fur. "I am glad to see that you are safe and well. But you have returned at a dangerous time. Shadow wants to lead the Moon-claw pack, but the others will not follow him while you live."

Storm's midnight-blue eyes flashed with anger. "Then perhaps it is time for me to face him!"

"Bravely said," Canista growled softly. "But you are not yet strong enough to overcome him and I am still too weak from Shadow's poisoned bite to help you. Use this puppy disguise. Go to the other world and hide. Return when your magic is stronger." As Canista finished speaking, she gasped with pain.

"Let me help you," Storm woofed, blowing out a cloud of golden sparkles. They swirled around Canista's paw for a moment before sinking into her fur and disappearing.

Canista gave a sigh of relief as a tiny bit of her strength returned.

Suddenly, another fierce howl rang out, sounding much closer. Heavy paws scraped at the rocks and Storm could hear harsh breathing.

"Shadow has found your scent! Go now, Storm. Save yourself!" Canista urged.

Storm whimpered as dazzling gold sparks ignited in his short brown-and-white puppy fur and he felt the power surging through him. The gold glow around him grew brighter. And brighter . . .

Chapter
ONE

Jessica Tennant stood on the doorstep, clutching a bag of her favorite DVDs as she listened to her best friend's mom.

"I'm afraid Sheena's in bed with a bad cold and a sore throat. I was just about to call you. It's a shame that your weekend's ruined. You'll have to come and stay another time."

"Oh well, she can't help being sick," Jessica said, trying hard to hide her disappointment. "I'd better go." She held out the bag of DVDs. "She can borrow these. Maybe they'll cheer her up. Will you tell Sheena that I hope she feels better soon?"

Sheena's mom smiled. "That's really nice of you, Jessica. Sheena will probably call you in a couple of days."

As the front door closed, Jessica's shoulders slumped. She slowly walked back to her parents who were waiting, parked outside in their van.

Mrs. Tennant looked at her daughter in surprise. "What's wrong? Why aren't you staying?" she asked.

Jessica shook her head. "Sheena's sick, so I can't stay. We were going to have a movie night and a midnight feast and everything. Now I don't know what to do," she said miserably.

"You'll just have to come with us

to the Balloon Festival," her mom
said.

Jessica made a face. She didn't want
to go to the boring Balloon Festival
with her parents. That's why she was
going to stay with Sheena in the first
place. "Can't I stay with Gran and
Gramps?"

"They're on vacation, remember?"
Mrs. Tennant said.

"Well, what about Anjum?" Jessica
said. "Oh, no . . . she's visiting her aunt.
I know! I think Gemma's at home. We
could ask—"

"Hang on, Jessica," her dad
interrupted. "I'm afraid we don't have
enough time to drive around to all
your friends' houses on the off chance
that you can stay with one of them. We
have to get going. The rest of the High
Flyers will already be on their way. Get
in, please."

"But . . ." Jessica's face fell as she
realized that she didn't have a choice.
Sighing heavily, she climbed into the
back and sat down. Leaning over, she

threw her overnight bag under the seat.

"Cheer up, Jess," her mom said, turning around to smile as Mr. Tennant pulled the van away from the curb and headed out of town. "I don't like to see you with such a long face."

Jessica felt so fed up, she could feel her face getting longer and longer. It would sag right onto the floor at this rate.

"You might even have a good time. You used to think that hot-air ballooning with us was pretty exciting," her mom said.

"Yeah! That was when I was little and before I knew that I seriously hated heights *and* found out that you had to hang around for hours when the weather's not right for flying.

Which is most of the time!" Jessica said bitterly.

Mrs. Tennant laughed. "You do exaggerate, Jessica Tennant! Anyway, the forecast's pretty good for this weekend."

Jessica wasn't excited by this news.

Mr. Tennant glanced at her in the rearview mirror. "You should be all right at Northampton. It's a really big festival. There'll be all kinds of stalls and displays and carnival rides to go on," he said cheerily.

"All by myself? Great," Jessica murmured through gritted teeth. She wished her mom and dad would stop trying to cheer her up. Nothing was going to make her feel better.

Crossing her arms, she slid down in her seat as they reached the highway and joined the endless stream of cars and trucks. Time seemed to crawl and the next two hours felt more like two weeks.

When they eventually reached the

festival, Jessica saw tons of people
putting up stalls, erecting tents, and
roping off display areas. Mr. Tennant
parked next to a shiny motor home
that was the size of a single-decker bus.
It made their van look very small.

"Look at that! It's even got its own
satellite dish!" Jessica said, impressed
despite herself.

"That's a Japanese model. They call
those RVs. I bet you could live in that
in the middle of a desert," her dad said.

"What's an RV?" Jessica asked.

"A recreational vehicle. I'd love one
of those!" her dad said.

"We'd have to sell the house first,"
Mrs. Tennant commented. She went
into the back of their van and began

getting things out for lunch. "Could
you go and get some water, please,
Jessica?"

Jessica picked up a container and
went trudging off across the parking lot.
She really wished Sheena was here. She
was missing her a lot.

As she walked past an empty
tent at the side of the parking lot,
Jessica spotted a girl coming toward her.
The girl looked about twelve,
two years older than Jessica, and she
was wearing a cool T-shirt and jeans.

Jessica smiled. This looked like
someone she might be able to make
friends with. "Hi!" she said as the girl
got closer. "Do you know where there's
a water fountain?"

"Do I look like I'd know?" the girl snapped.

"I guess not," Jessica said, thinking that she seemed very grumpy. Maybe her parents had forced her to come with them, too. "Are you here with a balloon club? I'm Jessica Tennant, by the way," she said, introducing herself.

"I'm Gayle Young. I'm with the Cloud Racers. It's the best club ever," the girl said, tossing her long brown hair over one shoulder.

"Dad says that about the High Flyers, too," Jessica joked. "That's the club we belong to."

"Huh! And I'm supposed to care?" Gayle murmured, poking at the grass with the toe of one expensive-looking sneaker.

Jessica's smile wavered, but she kept talking. "I saw some carnival rides and stuff on the way in. Maybe we could check them out together?" she suggested.

Gayle shrugged and wrinkled her nose. "No thanks. I'm not into hanging out with younger kids. I'm already stuck looking after Mikey—he's my little brother. I have to go now."

Jessica blushed as Gayle walked past her, disappointed that she was so unfriendly. "Well . . . er . . . good luck in the balloon races tomorrow, anyway," she called.

Gayle didn't bother to look back. "We

don't need luck. The Cloud Racers
always win," she drawled.

Jessica watched the older girl
walk over to the huge RV and

disappear inside it. "Oh gr-eat! Some weekend this is going to be!" she said to herself.

Jessica sighed and set off again to look for water. Suddenly, there was a flash of bright golden light and a crackle of sparks from the tent next to her.

She frowned. Jessica had briefly glanced inside as she passed and was sure she hadn't seen anything in there. But, she went to check anyway. As she had thought, there was only an upside-down cardboard box and some folded chairs lying on the grass.

Then Jessica noticed the tiny brown-and-white Jack Russell puppy sitting on the box. Its fur seemed to be gleaming as if it had been sprinkled with gold dust.

"Hello. What are you doing in there all by yourself?" she said, walking slowly toward the puppy so she didn't scare it.

"I come from far away. Can you help me, please?" the puppy woofed.

Chapter
* TWO *

Jessica stared at the puppy in utter amazement. She must be more upset by Gayle's unfriendliness than she thought. She'd just imagined that the tiny puppy had spoken to her!

"I am Storm, of the Moon-claw pack. What is your name?" the puppy yapped, looking up at her with an intelligent expression.

"Whoa! You *can* talk!" Jessica gasped, dropping the plastic water jug and taking a step backward. "Are you part of an act or something?"

She quickly poked her head outside
the tent's entrance to see if one of the
festival entertainers was outside and
playing a trick on her, but there was
no one there. Jessica turned back to
Storm. He was really cute with his soft
brown-and-white fur, tiny pointed face,
and the brightest midnight-blue eyes
she had ever seen.

Storm sat there with his ears pricked, looking at her quizzically as if expecting an answer.

"I'm J-Jessica Tennant," Jessica found herself stuttering. "I'm . . . here with my mom and dad for . . . for the Balloon Festival." She bent down and tried to make herself seem smaller so as not to alarm this amazing puppy. She still couldn't believe this was happening to her and she didn't want Storm to run away.

Storm dipped his head. "I am pleased to meet you, Jessica."

"Um . . . me too." Jessica blinked as she remembered something that Storm had just said. "What's the Moon-claw pack?"

"It is the wolf pack once led by my father and my mother," Storm told her proudly in a gruff little bark. "Shadow, the evil lone wolf, killed my father and three litter brothers and left my mother injured. He wants to lead the pack, but the others will not follow him while I am alive."

"Hang on! Did you say *wolf*? But you're a pu—"

"Please, stand back," Storm ordered, jumping down from the box.

There was another blinding flash and the air fizzed with gold sparks that fell harmlessly around Jessica and sizzled on the grass.

"Oh!" Jessica rubbed her eyes and when she could see again she noticed

that the tiny brown-and-white puppy
was gone. In its place there stood a
magnificent young silver-gray wolf
with thick fur and huge velvety paws
that seemed way too big for his body.
Despite being young, the wolf had
large sharp teeth and a thick neck-ruff
that glittered with big golden sparkles.

Jessica looked at it warily. "Storm?"

"Yes, it is me, Jessica. Do not be afraid," Storm growled softly.

But before Jessica had time to get used to the majestic young wolf, there was a final gold flash and Storm reappeared as a tiny helpless brown-and-white puppy.

"Wow! You really are a wolf. That's an amazing disguise!" Jessica said.

Storm began to tremble all over and his slender white tail drooped. "It will not save me if Shadow uses his magic to find me. I need to hide now. Can you help?" he asked.

Jessica's heart went out to him. She picked up the terrified puppy and pet his soft little head. "Of course I'll help you. You can live with m—"

She stopped as she remembered her

parents' strict rules about pets. "Oh, I'm not going to be allowed to keep you. Back home, everyone's out all day and most weekends, too. Mom and Dad don't think it's fair to leave a pet by itself."

"I understand. Thank you for your kindness, Jessica. I will find someone else who can help me," Storm woofed politely, beginning to walk away toward the tent opening.

"Wait!" Jessica called out urgently. She

wasn't ready to lose her new friend so
easily. Before he'd arrived she'd been
miserable. "There must be something I
can do. Maybe I could hide you in our
van. Except that it's really small and
Mom and Dad would probably find
you." She had a sudden thought. "Could
you pretend to be a toy dog? No, that

wouldn't work either, it would be too hard to stay really still and not even blink."

Storm looked up at her with bright midnight-blue eyes. "I can use my magic so that only you will be able to see and hear me."

"You can make yourself invisible? Cool! Then I don't have to worry about hiding you. You can sleep with me on the sofa bed at the end of the van."

"I would like that very much. Thank you, Jessica," Storm woofed. He leaned up and she felt his wet nose brush her chin as he began licking her face.

Jessica smiled down at the little puppy. She felt her heart lighten as she cuddled

Storm's warm furry body. Her lonely
boring weekend had just taken an
unexpected turn!

Chapter
* THREE *

Jessica and Storm sat at the table
under the awning, which her dad had
put up outside the camper van. The
other members of the High Flyers had
arrived now and they were all having
lunch together.

At first Jessica couldn't help worrying
that someone was going to see Storm
sitting on her lap, but when no one
noticed him, she began to relax. After
checking that she wasn't being watched,
Jessica broke off pieces of her cheese
sandwich and slipped them secretly to
Storm.

The tiny puppy chomped them up
eagerly and then jumped down onto
the grass. His tail wagged as he sniffed
the floor, licking up every last delicious
crumb. Jessica had to try really hard not
to giggle.

As soon as lunch was cleaned up,
Jessica's mom and dad and the other
High Flyers began unpacking the

balloon and equipment from a trailer.

Jessica had seen them do this hundreds of times. She was about to suggest to Storm that they go and take a walk, but he seemed fascinated by what was happening.

"What is that big flat colored object lying on the grass?" Storm woofed curiously as he ran around with his tongue hanging out. "Is it something to play with?"

"No! That's the club's balloon. It's made of a special light material but it's collapsed right now so you can't see the shape. Hey! Don't go running around on it or you'll get a big surprise!" she called to him in a whisper as Storm looked like he was about to pounce onto the balloon. "Once they've got the burner ready, they'll light the jets and start filling the balloon with hot air."

Storm's tiny forehead wrinkled in a furry frown. "What happens then?"

"The balloon inflates and gets really big. It's tied down now, but if it wasn't it would float right up in the air. As high as the clouds."

Storm glanced upward, his big bright eyes sparkling in amazement. "Up there?" he woofed.

Jessica nodded. She pointed to the basket that was lying next to the balloon. "See that? That's where Dad and the passengers stand when they go up in the balloon. You have to be a qualified pilot to be in charge. Dad's taken exams on flying and navigation and stuff. He's very experienced—he's won a lot of races!"

"But why do humans do this?" Storm wanted to know.

"It's a hobby. That's something you do for fun," Jessica explained.

Storm's midnight-blue eyes were as round as saucers—he couldn't believe that anyone would want to do such a strange thing. "Do *you* go up into the sky, Jessica?" he barked, looking very nervous.

"I used to, but I don't really like heights. My head feels really weird and I feel sick and dizzy," Jessica said. "I usually just watch from the ground or

go with Mom or someone else in the
support car to where the balloon lands.
Sometimes I stay in the van. But now
that you're here we can have fun
together."

Storm nodded, looking relieved, and
seemed to lose interest in the balloons.
"Does that mean lots of walks?" he
yapped, with a cute doggy grin.

"Definitely!" Jessica said, laughing.
"We can go for one now if you—"

There was a sudden loud hissing roar
as the burner ignited. A huge spurt of
bright-yellow flame shot out and heated
air began flowing into the collapsed
balloon.

"Yikes!" Storm yelped, almost
jumping out of his fur. He ran sideways

and his fur rose in a ridge along his little back. "Fire!"

Jessica felt a strange warm tingling feeling flowing down her spine as big gold sparks ignited in the tiny puppy's brown-and-white fur and his ears and tail crackled with electricity. Storm raised a front paw and a fountain of

gold glitter whooshed toward the burner.

There was a soft *phut!* and the gas jets went out.

Mr. Tennant looked puzzled. "That's weird. Maybe the jets need cleaning," he said, trying to light them again but without success.

"It's okay, Storm!" Jessica whispered quickly. "That's what's supposed to happen. Can you make the burner work again, please?"

Looking rather embarrassed, Storm sent more sparks shooting out of his paw. The jets lit immediately and a fresh burst of flame gushed out of them.

"That's it!" Mr. Tennant said.

Every last gold spark disappeared from Storm's fur, but Jessica could see that he was still frightened and shaky and his little white tail was drooping.

Jessica quickly checked that everyone was busy before pretending to bend down and tie her sneaker. "Don't worry. There's no danger. Dad knows a lot about health and safety," she soothed, petting Storm's soft little ears. "I'm sorry. I should have explained that the burners make a scary loud noise when you're not used to them."

Storm looked up at her trustingly and began wagging his tail.

Jessica felt a surge of affection for the brave little puppy who had stood his ground and tried to help her, despite his natural fear of fire.

"That's an ugly balloon! And the

basket's really small, isn't it?" said a familiar voice behind Jessica.

Gayle! Jessica jumped quickly to her feet, her heart racing in case the older girl had seen her talking to Storm. But Gayle was watching the blue, purple, and white balloon rippling as it swelled to its full size.

"It's big enough for us. Dad has won tons of trophies in it anyway," Jessica replied.

Gayle curled her lip. "Sure he has," she said, making it obvious that she didn't believe Jessica for a minute. Unexpectedly, she smiled and her voice softened. "Why don't you come and see our new balloon? It's *so* cool."

Jessica thought about reminding Gayle

that she'd said she didn't want to hang
out with younger kids, but her curiosity
got the best of her. "Okay then. We
might as well . . . um . . . I mean—
I might as well," Jessica corrected
quickly. She would have to be a lot
more careful about keeping Storm a
secret.

Gayle gave her a weird look, but then she smirked and turned on her heel.

As Jessica followed Gayle, Storm trotted beside her. They wove through the other balloons and trailers and came to a big open space.

A vast black balloon in the shape of a snarling wolf's head was almost drifting upright. It hung there, connected to an enormous basket and tied to the ground. Jessica stared at it in astonishment. She thought the basket could hold about ten people. The noise from the twin burners was really loud.

A gust of wind blew the huge black balloon and it seemed to turn in Jessica's direction and grin down at her like a fierce monster.

Storm laid his ears back, shot behind Jessica's legs, and stood there trembling.

"What did I tell you? Isn't it amazing?" Gayle said triumphantly.

"It's not bad," Jessica said, determined not to sound too impressed. The Cloud Racers seemed to be a much bigger club than the High Flyers. She could see about twenty people around the enormous balloon.

Jessica noticed a small boy standing with them. He looked about six years old and wore a bright-red Spider-Man T-shirt.

Gayle saw where she was looking. "That's my brother, Mikey. He's not allowed to go up in the balloon because the rules say he's too short. That's why he follows me around when Mom and Dad are flying. He's really annoying," Gayle grumbled.

Mikey looked over at Jessica and gave a bright smile. He seemed really sweet. *I don't think it's much fun for him either, having to put up with a sister like Gayle,* Jessica thought.

A blond woman stood next to Mikey. She looked over and waved at Gayle and Jessica. She was wearing a lot of bright makeup, a floaty pink top, and high-heeled sandals.

Gayle waved back. "That's my mom. Isn't she gorgeous? Just like a movie star."

"She's very pretty," Jessica commented, although she thought Mrs. Young

looked a little too dressed up for
ballooning. The other moms were
wearing shorts, T-shirts, and sneakers.

"If you've seen enough, you can go
back to your pathetic old balloon," Gayle
said cheerfully. She walked across the
grass toward her mom and little brother
without looking back.

Jessica's jaw dropped. She'd just given Gayle another chance to be friends and had ended up being ditched—again!

"Is there anybody as annoying as Gayle Young?" she complained to Storm. "Come on. I'll just go and tell my parents that I'm going for a walk."

"I would like that," Storm woofed. He threw a final scared glance at the monstrous black wolf balloon before scampering after Jessica.

Chapter
FOUR

"It's a no-fly evening," Mr. Tennant said with a sigh a couple of hours later as he came into the van.

Jessica was sitting reading a magazine on the sofa bed with Storm curled up beside her. They watched a monster truck display and then a circus workshop. Now the tiny puppy's ears were twitching as he slept and his tiny paws jerked as if he was running in his dreams.

As her dad came toward her, Jessica quickly shielded Storm with her

magazine and scooped him into her lap.

"Wroof!" the tiny puppy yapped in shock, instantly awake and alert.

"Sorry to disturb you, but Dad's about to squish you," Jessica whispered as her dad plopped down next to her, exactly where Storm had just been lying.

"Look at this sunny weather. You'd never think the wind conditions were bad for flying, would you?" Mr. Tennant complained.

Jessica didn't have the heart to remind him that this happened a lot on ballooning weekends, which was another reason why she was sometimes bored. But things were different for her now that she had such a special friend. Storm!

She smiled to herself as she imagined the look on her dad's face if he knew that there was an invisible magic puppy a few inches away from him.

"Never mind, Dad. There's still the

nightglow," she said to him, patting his arm. "People always love seeing the balloons lit up by the burners in the dark while they're still roped to the ground."

He smiled. "Well, you've cheered up. I

thought at one point you were going to be Miss Glum all weekend!"

"Da-ad! I wasn't that bad!" Jessica said. She gave him a friendly shove.

He grinned. "Says who? If your face had gotten any longer, you would have tripped right over it!"

Jessica couldn't help laughing. Her dad joined in.

After a few seconds, he wiped his eyes. "Well, since there's no race this evening, I'm going to start the barbecue. But first I'm going to have a cold drink and relax." He took a copy of *Balloon Life* magazine out of a nearby cabinet.

With her dad nearby, Jessica couldn't talk to Storm. She decided to take him for a short walk. "I think I might take another walk," she said to her dad.

Storm's ears pricked up immediately at the possibility of a walk. He jumped down with a soft *thud* and stood bright-eyed, wagging his tail hopefully.

Jessica smiled at him, feeling all light and happy. She realized that she wasn't missing Sheena that much anymore. She hoped her best friend wasn't feeling too sick.

Jessica and Storm set off in a roundabout way to avoid the tethered balloons and the noise of the gas burners, which Jessica knew still upset the little puppy.

They came to the biggest bouncy castle she had ever seen. It had dozens of towers and archways and things to climb on. There was even a giant slide. Kids were laughing and screaming as they bounced around having fun.

"Go on, you wimp. Just jump right onto it. It's not going to bite you!" cried an impatient voice.

It was Gayle and she was with her little brother.

"Gayle's with Mikey. Let's go and see what's going on," Jessica said to Storm.

Storm woofed softly in agreement.

"I don't want to get on it. There are too many big kids!" Gayle's little brother wailed, backing away.

Jessica could see that Mikey was close to tears but trying to hide it.

"You should have thought of that before I paid for a ticket!" Gayle complained. "It was out of my allowance money, too, and I bet I won't get that back. You're so annoying! Go on, Mikey. Get up there!"

"No-oooo! Leave me alone," Mikey sniffled.

Jessica felt herself getting angry. "Don't be mean, Gayle. He doesn't have to go on if he doesn't want to!" she said.

Gayle furiously turned around. "Who asked you to stick your nose in? Mikey's just chicken. *Cluck! Cluck!*" she mocked, flapping her arms.

"I'm not chicken! I'm not!" Mikey burst into tears.

Jessica's temper snapped. She glared at Gayle. "You're just a mean bully!" she burst out.

Gayle narrowed her eyes. "Who are you calling names?"

Jessica gulped as the older girl took a step toward her. Gayle suddenly seemed very tall and tough.

Storm softly growled a warning and

showed his sharp little teeth. Jessica felt another warm tingling sensation flowing down her spine.

Something very strange was about to happen.

Chapter
FIVE

As Jessica watched, big gold sparks
covered Storm's brown-and-white fur,
and his ears and tail fizzed with tiny
flashes of lightning. He raised a tiny
front paw and a spray of shimmering
glitter shot out and whizzed around
Gayle like a mini-tornado.

Gayle froze as the magical sparkles
whirled faster and faster. A strange, blank
expression came over her face. Suddenly,
she turned around, ran forward, and
jumped straight up onto the bouncy
castle.

Gayle did two small bounces and then on the third one she flew high into the air before doing a triple somersault. As soon as she landed she went straight up again, somersaulted, and twisted into two backflips.

The other kids stopped and watched her. They started clapping and cheering.

Mikey was no longer crying. His jaw dropped as he watched Gayle bouncing higher and higher, doing even more complicated jumps and twists.

"Aargh! What's happening?" Gayle cried, turning over and over, her arms spinning wildly and her legs working as if she was riding a bike.

"Hey! You! That's not allowed! Stop that at once!" the man in charge ordered, storming over.

"I can't! Help!" Gayle yelled, doing a handstand and another backflip. Suddenly, she did an extra-big bounce. She shot off the bouncy castle like a cork out of a bottle and landed on her feet a few feet away from Jessica. She stood there, swaying.

"I think I'm going to be sick," she groaned, her face looking green.

"Wow! That was awesome!" Mikey cried. "Watch me, Gayle!" He seemed to have lost all his nervousness as he jumped right onto the castle.

Gayle ignored him as she sank to the grass and sat there in a daze.

Jessica was trying hard not to laugh. "Storm!" she scolded gently.

Storm tucked his tail between his legs. "I am sorry. I think I used too much magic."

Jessica smiled at him. "Never mind. Maybe it'll teach Little Miss Bossy a lesson. And look at Mikey. He's really enjoying himself on the castle now! Come on, let's go for a walk."

Storm's midnight-blue eyes widened. "My favorite thing!"

Chapter
SIX

The delicious smell of barbecued sausages wafted toward Jessica as she and Storm walked back to the van about an hour later.

Her dad waved hello to her with a pair of tongs. He was wearing a new apron with a bright-green frog with big googly eyes on the front.

The other High Flyers were relaxing nearby in camping chairs and talking about hot-air ballooning as usual. They greeted Jessica and smiled at her as she and Storm went across to her mom, who was sitting at the table making a salad.

"Hello, sweetie. Did you have a good time?" Mrs. Tennant asked.

"Yeah, we saw some people dressed as moving statues and there was a magician, but it's starting to get really busy now and Storm was almost getting stepped on—" Jessica broke off. She couldn't believe that she'd been so careless! But luckily her mom was busy cutting up tomatoes and didn't seem to have heard. "I . . . um . . . got tired of pushing through the crowds," she finished.

Her mom nodded. "I suppose people are here for the nightglows and the fireworks. Do you want one hot dog or two?"

"Two please," Jessica said at once. *One for me and one for Storm*, she thought, hoping her mom wouldn't think she was being greedy!

She took her plate and went to sit on the grass while she ate. "Phew! That was close. I'm so bad at keeping secrets. I promise I'll get better!" she said to Storm.

Storm nodded as he chewed up his hot dog.

After they all finished eating, Jessica helped her mom clean up. The sky turned violet with pink streaks as the sun set and lights began turning on in the other motor homes. Her dad and the other High Flyers went to get the balloon ready for the nightglow.

"Should we go and watch?" Jessica's mom said, drying her hands.

"Okay. I'll follow you in a minute. I just want to get my bag. I think you'll be safer if you get inside it," she whispered to Storm.

Storm jumped right in with an eager little woof. As Jessica wandered across to the balloon display area, he settled down and poked out his head to look around.

The tethered balloons seemed dull and unimpressive against the evening sky, but at a signal all the burners were turned on. The balloons lit up, their beautiful colors shining green, gold, red, and blue, like glowing Chinese lanterns.

Storm yapped excitedly, forgetting to be nervous for a minute. "They are brighter than the Northern Lights that ripple across the sky in the long dark winter."

Jessica smiled, trying to imagine this wonderful sight. The other world where

Storm lived as a young wolf must be very strange and wonderful.

Jessica caught sight of Gayle walking toward them. "Uh-oh, here comes trouble," she whispered.

As Gayle reached Jessica's mom and dad, she gave them a huge smile. "Hi. Isn't it a beautiful evening," she called sweetly.

Jessica frowned. "Gayle is in a good mood. I wonder why."

"Hi! I came to find you. I thought you'd be watching the nightglow," Gayle said, smiling. She was twirling a necklace with a heart-shaped blue stone between her fingers. "Look what my dad just bought me. Do you like it?"

"It's really pretty," Jessica said.

Gayle smirked. "I know. Mom and Dad are really cool. They're always buying me presents. I bet you'd love a necklace like this."

Jessica shrugged. "Yeah, I guess. But, I usually only get presents on my birthday or for special occasions."

"Poor you. What a shame that your mom and dad don't have a lot of money. Anyone can tell that by looking at your dirty old van," Gayle commented.

"I like our van and it's not dirty! It's only got a few scratches," Jessica exclaimed, starting to get annoyed again. She made a huge effort to calm down. It just wasn't worth getting all annoyed at Gayle's pathetic comments.

"That was really weird on the bouncy castle earlier, wasn't it?" Gayle said.

Jessica shrugged. "I guess so," she said.

Gayle was watching her closely. "I don't know what happened, but I bet you had something to do with it. I didn't think you had it in you," she said.

Jessica looked at Gayle in surprise and wondered whether she could actually be fun underneath it all.

"You just loved seeing me make a fool out of myself, didn't you?" Gayle commented.

"Well, it was pretty funny," Jessica said and then wished she hadn't. Gayle scowled and the familiar mean look came over her face. She wasn't being friendly at all now—maybe she had just been pretending.

"You think you're so cool, don't you?" Gayle spat. "Well, no one makes fun of me and gets away with it! Just remember that!"

As Gayle stomped off, Jessica looked

down at Storm with concern. "What do you think she means?"

Storm frowned at her from the bag. "It sounded as if she is going to try and get you back."

"Well, let her try!" Jessica said. "We'll be ready, won't we?"

She reached into her bag to pet Storm's smooth warm fur and didn't notice the concerned look on his tiny face.

Chapter
SEVEN

"There it is! That's our balloon!" Jessica cried early the following morning, pointing to a bead-sized blue dot high in the sky.

Storm sat on Jessica's lap in the back of the the High Flyers' support car. Kim, who owned the car, was driving. Jessica's mom was in the passenger seat with a map and instruments on her lap. They were carefully tracking the balloon, so that they would be in exactly the right spot to help with the landing.

"Grr–uff! Grr–uff!" Storm barked as he jumped up onto his hind legs and poked his nose out of the open window.

"Careful, Storm. Make sure you don't fall out," Jessica cautioned in a whisper.

It was 6:30 A.M. and conditions were

perfect for ballooning. The clear blue
sky overhead seemed filled with layers
of balloons of all shapes and sizes.

"Just look at that one!" Jessica said,
pointing to a giant rabbit that seemed
to be waving its paw. She could see a
can of soup and a big smiling head
wearing earphones, but her favorite was
a crocodile eating a packet of crackers.

"They are like giant creatures that
roar and spit fire and chase each
other!" Storm yapped. He still wasn't
used to the burners. A tiny growl
rumbled in his throat whenever the
hissing roar of one of them echoed on
the still air.

"They're just dumb old sacks of
hot air. They won't hurt you," Jessica

soothed, petting his tense little body.

Storm gradually started to relax as Kim headed out into the countryside and drove through villages. By the time they were getting close to a patchwork of open fields, Jessica could see that the High Flyers' balloon was beginning to drift downward.

"They'll be coming down in the fields somewhere over here," Mrs. Tennant judged, pointing at a map with her pencil. "We should go right at the next crossroads."

"Got it," Kim said, concentrating hard.

"This is the tricky part," Jessica whispered to Storm. "Landing can be dangerous because of power lines and stuff. Sometimes the ground wind's too strong and the basket tips over and the balloon drags it along."

"That is not good. Someone could get hurt," Storm woofed worriedly.

"Yes, but Dad's a great pilot. You'll see. Here they come! Look!" Jessica waved to her dad, who was just a tiny figure in the basket at that moment.

Minutes later, Kim stopped the car and everyone got out. Jessica and Storm followed her mom and Kim across an unplowed field.

Suddenly, a huge black wolf balloon rose up from behind some tall trees and began descending rapidly.

Jessica ducked instinctively. "It's the Cloud Racers! They're going to land,

too, but they're really close to our
balloon!"

Storm gave a piercing whine of
terror. He ran forward and hurtled
across the field in a blind panic.

"Storm!" Jessica gasped. He must have

thought that the monster balloon was about to attack him.

"Where did that puppy come from?" her mom cried.

Jessica realized that Storm was so scared that he must have forgotten to stay invisible. He wouldn't be able to use his magic to save himself without giving himself away!

Without a second thought, Jessica shot across the field after him. Her heart pounded as she ran and her sneakers got covered in the muddy soil. The Cloud Racers' enormous black balloon seemed to blot out the entire sky and the huge basket was barely five feet above her head. Glancing upward, Jessica caught a glimpse of horrified faces looking down at her.

Storm froze. He didn't seem to realize that he was right in the balloon's path. His midnight-blue eyes were like saucers and his fur stood up along his back.

In desperation, Jessica threw herself forward. Her fingers brushed Storm's brown-and-white fur. Yes! She grabbed the tiny puppy and held him to her chest and then rolled over and over with him, as she'd been taught to do in gym class at school.

Just as she came to a stop beside the fence at the side of the field, she smashed her knee on a large half-buried stone. "Oh!" she gasped as a sharp pain took her breath away.

"Look out!" Jessica's mom and Kim were running across the field frantically waving their arms at the huge black balloon.

Jessica heard a shout from overhead. The powerful burners roared out and the monster wolf balloon slowed. For an agonizingly long moment, it seemed to hang in the air and then it rose just high enough to sweep over her and Storm and skim the fence into the next field.

Jessica lay there, holding the shocked puppy. Her entire leg seemed to be aching and she couldn't move.

She saw her dad steering their balloon to a safe landing, thirty feet away across the field. Kim ran to catch the anchor rope, while Jessica's mom ran to where Jessica lay.

"Jessica! Are you all right?" Mrs. Tennant shouted anxiously.

"I'm okay, Mom. Just a little shaken up," Jessica cried.

Storm barked and reached up to lick Jessica's face. "Thank you for saving me. You were very brave."

"I wasn't really. I didn't think about it, but I just knew that I couldn't bear anything to happen to you. Quick, you'd better become invisible again. Mom's almost here!" Jessica said, wincing.

"You have hurt yourself! I will make you better," Storm woofed.

Jessica felt the familiar tingling down her spine as Storm opened his mouth and huffed out a cloud of tiny gold sparks as fine as gold dust. The glittering mist

swirled around Jessica's leg. The pain in
her knee felt very hot for a second and
then it turned ice cold and completely
drained away like water gurgling down
a drain.

"Thanks, Storm. I'm fine now," she
said, quickly putting him on the ground

and getting to her feet just as her mom reached her.

"You crazy girl! Whatever made you run after that puppy? You could have been really hurt!" Mrs. Tennant screamed, looking red-faced and shaky. "Where is the little puppy, anyway?"

"It . . . er . . . ran away through the h-hedge," Jessica mumbled hurriedly. "It must have been a stray. Anyway, I'm all right, Mom. Don't worry!"

"Jessica Tennant . . ." her mom said darkly, looking as if she was about to make a very big scene.

Jessica swallowed and decided that it might be best to change the subject. "Shouldn't we go and help Dad and the others?" she said quickly.

With Storm following her, she marched across the field to where Kim, her dad, and the others were dealing with the balloon.

Chapter
EIGHT

That evening, the weather was perfect and the balloons were flying. Jessica decided to stay behind with Storm this time. She found a booth selling cotton candy and then one selling pet food and bought him a dog treat.

They went over toward the old pavilion, where it wasn't so crowded, to sit on the grass and eat.

"When do we go back to your home place, Jessica?" Storm woofed around a crunchy mouthful.

"Tomorrow. There's another race at

6 A.M. and then the award ceremony.
After that we'll go home," she replied.
"I can't wait for you to meet Sheena.
She's going to love you!"

"I am sorry, Jessica, but you cannot
tell anyone about me. Not even your
friend." Storm's big dewy blue eyes
were serious.

"Oh." Jessica felt disappointed that she
couldn't even tell her best friend about
Storm, but if that would keep him safe,
she didn't mind too much.

Jessica ate the last of her cotton candy.
She licked her fingers and stood up.
"Finished?" she said to Storm.

Storm nodded. He leaped to his feet
and ran across the well-kept grass.

An old candy wrapper blew around

and Storm's bright eyes sparked with
mischief as he pounced on it. Tossing
his head from side to side, he ran
around with the wrapper in his mouth.

Jessica smiled at his cute antics.
Sometimes it was hard to believe that
the adorable puppy was really a majestic

young silver-gray wolf who would one day lead his pack.

Suddenly, Storm stopped. He stood there quivering with concentration for a few seconds and then gave a loud yelp of terror and bolted straight into a flower bed.

Jessica stiffened. But she couldn't see what had frightened Storm. What could be wrong? She raced over to the flower bed and began searching beneath a flowering bush.

"Storm? Where are you?" she called anxiously.

At first she couldn't see any sign of the little puppy, but then she spotted him. He was tucked in a tight ball in a space between two drooping branches.

"Is this a game or something? Oh, I get it. You're playing a trick on me!" she said, smiling, but then her face got serious when she saw that he was trembling all over.

"I saw a huge dog over by that tree. I think Shadow has used his magic to turn it into a wolf and send it after me!" Storm whined.

Jessica felt really scared. If Storm's enemy had found him, the tiny puppy was in terrible danger.

She glanced anxiously toward the tree and saw a woman with a big German shepherd dog on a leash. The dog saw her looking and its tongue lolled in a friendly doggy grin.

"Those dogs kind of look like wolves,

but that one seems gentle," Jessica whispered uncertainly as the woman and her dog came closer. "How will I know if it's under a magic spell?"

"It will have fierce pale eyes and extra-long sharp teeth," Storm whined nervously.

Jessica looked at the German shepherd again. "It doesn't look like that. I think it's okay."

Storm crawled forward with his belly close to the ground and his tail between his legs. He peered through the drooping branches at the big dog and Jessica saw him gradually relax.

"You are right. I am wrong this time. But if Shadow finds me, he *will* use his magic to hunt me down."

Jessica felt like she needed to comfort
Storm. She bent down and picked
Storm up as he crept out from under
the bush. She could feel his little heart
beating fast against her fingers. "I hope
that horrible Shadow never finds you
and then you can come home with me
and stay forever!"

Storm looked up at her. "One day, I must return to my own world to help my mother and become leader of the Moon-claw pack. Do you understand that, Jessica?" he yapped gently.

Jessica nodded, but she didn't want to think about that right now. "That was pretty scary. Let's go back to the van and spend some quiet time together," she said, changing the subject.

Storm reached up to lick her chin. "I would like that," he barked.

Jessica carried Storm to the parking lot. As they got closer to their van, they saw the door open and a girl peering out. After she quickly looked around, she climbed down and hurried away.

"That was Gayle. What's she doing in our van?" Jessica wondered.

Storm frowned. "I do not know."

"Maybe Mom came back to get something and Gayle was talking to her," Jessica said, knowing how Gayle was always careful to be on her best behavior around adults.

But when she went inside, she saw that the van was empty.

Storm stood with his head to one side.

"What is it?" Jessica asked him.

"Something is different . . ." Tiny gold sparks began twinkling in Storm's fur and his wet brown nose began to glow like a gold nugget. With a triumphant woof he jumped up onto the back seat and began searching behind a cushion. A moment later, he emerged holding something in his mouth.

It was a gold necklace with a blue, heart-shaped stone.

Jessica recognized it. "That's Gayle's new necklace. She must have put it there. But why?"

"I think I know why!" Storm barked and then he pricked up his ears. "Someone is coming!" He picked up the necklace and dashed out of the open door with it in his mouth.

Puzzled, Jessica followed hard on his heels. "Storm? What's going on? Where are you go—" she started to ask and then stopped herself quickly as she saw

Gayle and her mom standing there.

Mrs. Young was wearing a frilly blue dress and high heels. She had one arm around Gayle, who was dabbing at her eyes with a tissue.

"I want a word with you, young lady!" Mrs. Young said at once. "Gayle lost her new necklace and she thinks that you might know something about it!"

"Me?" Jessica said, almost speechless.

Gayle grinned slyly. "Don't try and look innocent," she sniffled. "I know you took it."

Jessica couldn't believe her ears. "I couldn't care less about your stupid necklace. I didn't take it!" she burst out.

"Huh! You would say that!" Gayle sneered. "I bet you've hidden it inside

the van. Come on, Mom, let's go inside
and look for it."

"Now wait just a minute!" said a deep
voice behind them.

"Dad!" Jessica gave a cry of relief as
her dad stepped forward.

"I heard all that," he said. "And I can
assure you that my daughter's no thief. If
Jessica says she didn't take the necklace, I
believe her."

Mrs. Young gave him a charming smile. Her teeth were very white against her bright-pink lipstick. "In that case, you won't mind if we come into your van and have a look."

"I certainly do mind! Gayle probably dropped that necklace somewhere. I suggest you go and look for it, before you come here making wild accusations," Mr. Tennant said calmly.

"Well! If that's your attitude," Mrs. Young said indignantly, drawing herself up. "You haven't heard the last of this, I assure you. Come along, Gayle."

Gayle looked as if she was about to object, but she turned and hurried after her.

As Mrs. Young walked toward her

motor home in her high heels, she
suddenly stopped. "What's that glinting
in the grass?" she said, bending down to
pick something up. She turned to Gayle.
"It's your necklace! You must have
dropped it, just like Mr. Tennant said."

"But I don't get it! I put it under . . .
I mean . . . I . . . um . . . didn't . . ."
Gayle stammered in confusion.

"You've made me look a complete
idiot!" Mrs. Young fumed, marching
Gayle up the steps of the RV. "What
have you been up to? And you'd better
tell me the truth, or you'll be
grounded!"

The door closed firmly and
everything was silent. Jessica guessed
that Gayle was getting a really severe

lecture. She turned back to her dad. "Thanks for sticking up for me, Dad."

"No problem," he said, giving her shoulder a squeeze. "You haven't got a mean bone in your body, Jessica Tennant. But it was a good thing we got back here in time."

Just as her dad went into the van, Storm came out from underneath the van and ran up to Jessica.

"Thanks, Storm. That was a great idea to drop Gayle's necklace over by the RV. It really turned the tables on her!"

"You are welcome, Jessica. I do not think she will be making any more trouble," he yapped happily.

Chapter
NINE

Jessica woke up early on Sunday morning. Pale lemon sunlight was just pushing through the crack in the van's curtains.

Storm was lying next to her. He wagged his little tail as she pet him, and snuggled back under the warm blanket with a contented sigh.

Even though it was early, Jessica was wide awake. Leaving Storm lying there, she carefully climbed over him and dressed in shorts and a T-shirt. After boiling some water for tea, she brought

her mom and dad a cup of tea in bed.

"Thanks, sweetie. You're an early bird today!" Mr. Tennant sat up looking sleepy-eyed and with his hair all messy. "You're not making breakfast, too, are you?" he asked hopefully.

Jessica took the hint. "Eggs on toast?"

By the time they were cleaning up

the cups and plates, the other High Flyers had arrived. Kim had bad news.

"It's going to be another no-fly day," she announced. "So the winning times have been worked out from Friday's and Saturday's flights. We're in second place. The Cloud Racers are first."

Mr. Tennant nodded. "Ah well, that's how it goes," he said good-naturedly. "It's a shame we won't get a chance for another flight. But there'll still be a balloon tether before we pack up for good."

"That's when the balloons are roped to the ground and just hover a few inches in the air. No balloon monsters high in the sky to scare you today,"

Jessica explained in a whisper to Storm.

Outside in the enclosure, cars and trailers had parked and the grass was already covered with acres of brightly colored nylon. Jessica could see that the Cloud Racers' basket lay on its side. The burners were going and the huge black wolf face was almost fully inflated.

She and Storm were standing with her mom and dad when Gayle's parents approached them. Mrs. Young was holding Mikey's hand.

"Have you seen Gayle?" Mr. Young asked Jessica.

Jessica shook her head, puzzled. "No, I haven't seen her since yesterday."

She noticed that Mrs. Young looked different and then realized why. Gayle's

mom was in jeans and a crumpled
T-shirt and she wasn't wearing make-up.
Her eyes looked puffy as if she'd been
crying.

"Is something wrong?" Mrs. Tennant
asked her gently.

"It's Gayle. She's missing," Mrs. Young
said with a shaky voice. "We had a bit

of a fight about this necklace business. I thought at first that she'd gone off somewhere sulking by herself—she's done it before. But it's been over an hour now and I'm starting to get really worried."

"I'll help you look for her," Jessica offered at once.

"That's very nice of you, especially after the way Gayle behaved," Mr. Young said.

"Anyone can make a mistake," Jessica said generously.

"Let's all spread out and look around," Mr. Tennant suggested.

"Good idea. I'll look over here," Jessica said, walking off with Storm. She waited until her mom and dad had gone in opposite directions and then turned to Storm. "Do you think you can pick up Gayle's scent?" she asked.

"I will try," Storm woofed.

Scampering over to the Youngs' RV, he began sniffing around in the grass.

Jessica followed him and watched as he worked his way back and forth. Moments later, his head came up. "This way," he yapped triumphantly.

Jessica ran after him as he headed toward the line of tethered balloons. The Cloud Racers' huge black balloon and basket were floating a few inches above the ground. Two of the club members were standing with their backs to the balloon.

Jessica caught a sudden movement

from the corner of her eye. A slim
figure suddenly dashed out from behind
a van and quick as a flash scrambled
unseen into the huge basket.

"It's Gayle!" Jessica gasped, rushing
forward with Storm at her heels.

As she ran up to the balloon, she saw
Gayle lean over, unhook a rope, and
drop it to the ground. The basket
wobbled and tipped at a crazy angle.

The two club members turned. They
realized what was happening and
quickly grabbed a rope each, but the
balloon began to rise slowly as Gayle
unhooked another rope and threw it
down.

"Gayle, don't!" Jessica cried.

Gayle glared at her. "What do you

care? You don't like me. Everyone hates me!" The balloon rose up higher, almost free.

"I don't hate you, and your mom and dad are really worried about you. Just stay still and let the team get you down," Jessica pleaded.

Gayle bit her lip and looked as if she might be starting to believe Jessica.

"Gayle! What on earth do you think you're doing? Get down from there!" Mr. Young ordered as he, his wife, and Mikey ran toward the balloon.

Then everything happened at once.

The club members, already on tiptoe and trying to hold down the balloon, were lifted off their feet. They dropped to the ground as the black balloon rose into the air, trailing ropes and taking Gayle up with it.

Jessica saw the balloon ripple as if it was caught in a side wind. It lurched sideways and the wolf face seemed to leer as it started to collapse.

Gayle screamed and clung on to the basket.

Jessica gasped in horror. The whole thing was going to come crashing down!

Chapter
TEN

Time seemed to stand still.

Huge gold sparks bloomed in Storm's
brown-and-white fur and his ears
fizzed with power. He shot into the air,
with a comet's tail of sparkles behind him,
and landed in the basket next to Gayle.

Jessica saw a burst of flame shoot out of the gas jets. Hot air flowed into the balloon, which swelled out and straightened itself. At the same time a gush of gold sparkles erupted in the basket, and ropes snaked downward toward the ground.

Eager hands reached for them and they were quickly secured. People ran to help and the balloon was drawn downward until the basket rested on the grass.

Jessica saw Storm leap out and streak toward her.

Gayle's dad leaped into the basket and gave his daughter a huge hug. "Are you all right, sweetie? I was terrified that you were going to be hurt. Thank goodness that you had the sense to work the burner and throw down those extra ropes."

Gayle was white-faced. She didn't seem to know whether to laugh or cry. "Burner? But I . . ." she stammered shakily.

But her dad wasn't listening. He helped Gayle climb out of the basket and one of the club members reached forward to help her. Everyone cheered and clapped.

Gayle hung her head and chewed at her lip. "Thanks, everyone. I-I didn't mean for that to happen. I'm glad that no one got hurt because of me."

Jessica could see that, for once, Gayle really meant it.

She looked down at Storm who stood beside her. Every last spark had faded from his fur. She wished she could cuddle him, but there were too many people around for her to pick him up.

"That was incredibly brave of you to light the burner, Storm. I know how fire scares you," she whispered.

"I am just glad that Gayle is safe. But I do not think I will ever grow to like hot-air balloons," he barked.

Jessica noticed Gayle looking at her in a very strange way. She realized that the older girl had heard her whispering to Storm!

Gayle smiled knowingly and then she shrugged. "Weird things keep happening

when you're around, Jessica. I'd love to
know what's been going on, but I guess
I never will. Keep your secrets. It's fine
by me. And thanks for trying to help
me. I'm sorry for being such a pain.
Can we start all over again and try to
be friends?"

"I'd like that," Jessica replied, pleased.

"Cool! Why don't you come over to our RV? You haven't seen inside yet, right? It's got a huge shower room and a TV and everything."

Jessica smiled. Gayle would never change, but at least she was trying to be a lot nicer now. "Okay, thanks. I'd love to see inside it," she said.

Gayle beamed at her. She reached for Mikey's hand before walking off with her parents. "See you in a minute, Jessica."

With the excitement over, people began dispersing. Suddenly, Storm whimpered and began trembling all over. He took off like a rocket and headed toward a clump of thick bushes a few feet away.

"I'll . . . I'll be right back!" Jessica said to her mom. She hurtled after the terrified puppy, a terrible suspicion rising in her mind.

She spotted three dogs running toward the bushes from the opposite direction. They had fierce pale eyes and extra-long sharp teeth. Shadow had put a spell on them. They were here for Storm.

As Jessica pushed her way into the center of the bushes there was a dazzling flash of bright gold light.

Storm stood there; he was no longer a tiny brown-and-white Jack Russell puppy. He was a majestic young wolf with thick silver-gray fur. A thousand tiny gold diamonds sparkled in his neck-ruff. Beside him stood an older she-wolf with a gentle expression on her face.

At that moment, Jessica knew that Storm must leave her. Her throat clenched with sadness, but she forced herself to be brave. "Save yourself, Storm!" she cried.

"Be of good heart, Jessica. You have

been a loyal friend," Storm said in a deep velvety growl.

There was a final burst of intense gold light, and a silent explosion of sparks crackled down around Jessica. Storm and his mother faded and were gone.

There was a growl of rage as the fierce dogs burst through the bushes. Seeing that Storm had disappeared, their eyes and teeth instantly returned to normal and they fled.

Jessica felt stunned. It had all happened so fast. Her heart was aching, but at least she'd had a chance to say good-bye. Storm was safe and she hoped that one day he would be able to stay in his own world and lead the Moon-claw pack.

Tears pricked her eyes as she slowly

began walking back toward the parking lot. Jessica knew she would never forget her wonderful adventure with Storm.

She thought of Sheena and hoped she was feeling better. Jessica decided to buy her a cuddly toy to cheer her up. Then she smiled as she saw Gayle waiting for

her. Perhaps she'd get Gayle one, too. A cute toy puppy for both of them.

After all, she thought, *everyone should have their own magic puppy.*

About the Author

Sue Bentley's books for children often include animals, fairies, and wildlife. She lives in Northampton and enjoys reading, going to the movies, relaxing by her garden pond, and watching the birds feeding their babies on the lawn. At school she was always getting yelled at for daydreaming or staring out of the window—but she now realizes that she was storing up ideas for when she became a writer. She has met and owned many cats and dogs, and each one has brought a special kind of magic to her life.

Read all of the other books
in the Magic Puppy series!

#1 A New Beginning

#2 Muddy Paws

#3 Cloud Capers

#4 Star of the Show